R U B Y

For Ellie, Naomi, Roddy
and special bears everywhere

A Red Fox Book

Published by Random House Children's Books
20 Vauxhall Bridge Road, London SW1V 2SA.

A division of Random House UK Ltd
London Melbourne Sydney Auckland
Johannesburg and agencies throughout the world

First published in 1990 by
Hutchinson Children's Books

Red Fox edition 1992

7 9 10 8

Printed in Singapore

Random House Limited Reg. No. 954009

RUBY

Maggie Glen

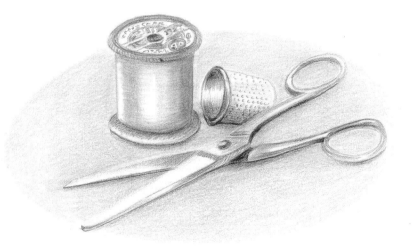

RED FOX

Ruby felt different from other bears – sort of special.

Mrs Harris had been day-dreaming when she
made Ruby. She didn't notice that she'd used
the spotted material that was meant for the toy leopards.
She didn't watch carefully when she sewed on
the nose.

Ruby wasn't surprised when she was chosen
from the other bears, but she didn't like
being picked up by her ear.

'OUCH, GET OFF!' she growled.

Ruby's paw was stamped with an 'S' and she was thrown into the air.

'YIPEE - E - E - E! "S" IS FOR SPECIAL,' yelled Ruby.

Ruby flew across the factory and landed in a box full of bears.

'Hello,' she said. 'My name's Ruby and I'm special – see.'

She held up her paw.

'No silly,' laughed a big bear. ' "S" is for second – second best.'
'We're mistakes,' said the bear with rabbit ears.
'When the box is full, we'll be thrown out.'
Ruby's fur stood on end; she was horrified.

More bears joined them in the box.

At last the machines stopped.

They listened to the workers as they chatted and hurried to catch the bus home.

They heard the key turn in the lock.

Then everything was quiet.

One by one the bears fell asleep.

All except Ruby – Ruby was thinking. The only sound was the sound of the big bear snoring.

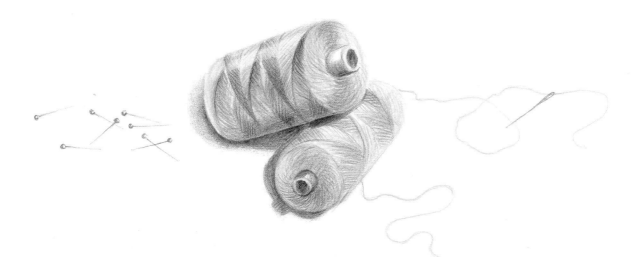

Hours passed. Suddenly Ruby shouted, 'That's it!'
'What's it?' gasped the rabbit-eared bear
who woke up with a fright.
'Zzzzzzzzzzzzzzzzz-w-w-what's going on?'
groaned the big bear, rubbing his sleepy eyes.
'That's *it*,' said Ruby again. 'We'll escape.'

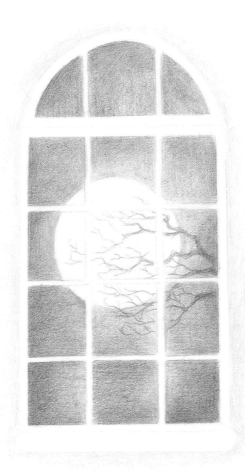

'ESCAPE!' they all shouted. And they jumped out of the box.

'Let's go!' said Ruby.

They looked for a way out.

They rattled the windows.

They pushed at the doors.

'There *is* no way out,' cried a little bear. 'We're trapped.'

'This way,' shouted Ruby, rushing into the cloakroom.

They found a broken air vent.

It was a very tight squeeze. They pushed and they pulled, they wiggled and they waggled, until they were all in the yard outside.

They ran silently, swiftly, through the night and into the day.

Some ran to the country, some to the town.

Some squeezed through letterboxes.   Some slipped through open windows.

Some hid in toy cupboards.

Some crept into bed with lonely children.

But Ruby . . .

. . . climbed into the window of the very best toy shop in town.

The other toys stared at Ruby.

  'What's the "S" for?' squealed the pigs.

  'Special,' said Ruby, proudly.

  All the toys shrieked with laughter.

  'Scruffy,' said the smart-looking penguin.

  'Soppy,' said the chimpanzee.

  'Stupid,' giggled the mice.

  'Very strange for a bear,' they all agreed.

'Don't come next to me,' said a prim doll.

'Wouldn't want to,' said Ruby.

'Stand at the back,' shouted the other toys.

They poked, they pulled, they prodded and they pinched. Ruby pushed back as hard as she could, but there were too many of them.

So Ruby spent all day at the back of the shelf.

Then, just before closing time, a small girl came into the shop with her grandfather.

They searched and searched for something – something different, something special.

'That's the one,' said the little girl.

'Yes, Susie,' said Grandfather, 'that one looks very special.'

Ruby looked around her. 'Can they see me?'

'IT'S ME! They're pointing at me. WHOOPEE-E-E-E!'
'We'll have that one, please,' said Grandfather.

The shopkeeper put Ruby on the counter.
She looked at the 'S' on Ruby's paw.
'I'm sorry, sir,' she said, 'this one is a second. I'll fetch another.'

'No thank you, that one is just perfect,' said Grandfather. 'It has character.'

Character, thought Ruby, that sounds good.

'Shall I wrap it for you?' the shopkeeper asked.

'Not likely,' growled Ruby. 'Who wants to be shoved in a paper bag?'

'No thank you,' said Susie. 'I'll have her just as she is.'

They all went out of the shop and down the street.

When they came to a yellow door they stopped.

'We're home, Spotty,' said Susie.

'SPOTTY, WHAT A CHEEK!' muttered Ruby.

'It's got a growl,' said Susie, and she and her grandfather laughed.

Susie took off her coat and scarf and sat Ruby on her lap.

Susie stared at Ruby and Ruby stared back.

Suddenly, Ruby saw a little silver "S"
hanging on a chain round Susie's neck.

Hooray! thought Ruby. One of us – a special.